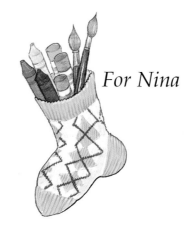

For Nina

Library of Congress Cataloging-in-Publication Data

Szekeres, Cyndy.
　　Yes, Virginia, there is a Santa Claus / adapted and illustrated by Cyndy Szekeres.
　　　p. cm.
　　Summary: Virginia O'Hanlon, a young cat, questions a major New York newspaper about the existence of Santa Claus and she receives an answer from the paper's editor that reaffirms the spirit of Christmas.
　　ISBN 0-590-69196-1
　　1. Santa Claus — Juvenile fiction. [1. Santa Claus — Fiction. 2. Cats — Fiction.]
I. Church, Francis Pharcellus, 1839-1906. Yes, Virginia, there is a Santa Claus. II. Title.
PZ7.S988Ye　1997
[E]—dc21
96-48181
CIP
AC

JCHRISTMAS
52E
C. 1

10　9　8　7　6　5　4　3　2　1
Printed in Singapore　　46
First printing, November 1997

Yes, Virginia
There Is a Santa Claus

Adapted and Illustrated by
Cyndy Szekeres

Cartwheel
·B·O·O·K·S·® SCHOLASTIC INC.
New York Toronto London Auckland Sydney

This letter was once received by the editor of the *New York Sun*, a daily newspaper published in the late 1800s in New York City.

> *Dear Editor,*
> *I am 8 years old. Some of my friends say there is no Santa Claus. Papa says, "If it's printed in the* Sun, *it's so." Please tell me the truth. Is there a Santa Claus?*
>
> *Virginia O'Hanlon*

And the editor answered...

Yes, Virginia, there is a Santa Claus. He exists, just as love, generosity, and friendship exist—and you know that those things are everywhere and they bring you happiness every day.

Not believe in Santa Claus? You might as well not believe in fairies!

You may ask your papa to hire people to catch Santa Claus. But even if they did not see Santa coming down the chimney, what would that prove?

Nobody sees Santa Claus.

But nobody can find proof that there is no
Santa Claus, either.

The most real things in the world are
those that neither children nor
grown-ups can see.

Did you ever see fairies dancing on the lawn? Of course not! But that doesn't prove that they are not there.

Nobody can conceive of or imagine
all the wonders that are unseen and
unseeable in the world.

No Santa Claus!

Be thankful that he lives...

...and he lives forever.

A thousand years from now, Virginia,

no, even ten thousand years from now,

he will continue…

...to make glad the hearts of children.